Part of an oil painting by John Leigh-Pemberton demonstrating the degree of detail that can be achieved in oils.

D1498334

Left are two contrasting styles of water-colour painting by Rowland Hilder (above) and Stanley Badmin (below).

A typical use of gouache colour in a technical illustration by Gerald Witcomb.

Many people want to paint pictures but don't know where to start. This book introduces the three basic types of paint – gouache, water-colour *and* oil paint *– and outlines the brushes and painting surfaces needed by a beginner. Each section gives basic techniques and ideas which can be explored by beginner painters to give confidence, inspiration and lots of enjoyment to aspiring artists.*

Acknowledgments
The picture of Van Gogh's painting, *A Cornfield, with Cypresses,* on page 50 is reproduced by courtesy of the Trustees, The National Gallery, London. The pictures on page 10 are by Stanley Bell (top) Philip Thompson (bottom right) and Douglas Kemp (bottom left).

The publishers would like to thank George Rowney and Sons for supplying painting materials used in the preparation of this book.

Painting

*written and illustrated
by* KATHIE LAYFIELD

with contributions by
JENNY COOK & FRANK HUMPHRIS

photographs by
TIM CLARK

Ladybird Books Loughborough

Introduction

Have you ever looked at a picture and thought 'I'd like to do one like that', or perhaps you've been given some paints and, although you really want to use them, you just don't know where to begin?

Initially, try not to think about doing paintings to hang on the wall for everyone to see. The pictures you make are your personal statements about a subject. If someone else likes them later, then that's an extra bonus.

First of all you will need to discover, by experimenting, the different ways of using your paints.

Every type of paint has its own special qualities and it is only by experimenting with them that you will come to understand them. Some paints, like poster colours, powder colours and designers' gouache, are best used *thickly* at a creamy consistency. Oil paint and acrylic colours can be used either thickly or in transparent form.

Try painting a picture using as many varieties of one colour as you can find. Sometimes you will find different examples amongst the paints you have bought, but many more can be achieved by mixing colours together.

Learning how to mix colours to create new ones is a very important aspect of painting. Many colours can be mixed from only red, blue and yellow. These are known as the *primary* colours and your range of colours will be extended if you use black and white to darken or lighten them to create shades or tones.

If you add black to a colour it may surprise you to discover that it doesn't just darken it but will often give another colour entirely. For example, yellow with a little black gives a green colour; red with black makes a brown or purple colour. This is because black paint contains blue *pigments*.

This array of colours is the result of mixing only the three primary colours (red, blue and yellow) with black and white.

When you mix two or more colours together, notice how the colours change their mood. A red with yellow in it seems warmer and happier than a red with blue in, which is cooler and more serious. Green with some yellow is a fresh colour, like Spring and growing plants, whereas green with red in it gives a browny colour, more like Autumn. If you then add a touch of blue you produce a darker and more sombre colour altogether.

In general we can say that reds, oranges and yellows are 'warm' colours, because we associate them with fire and strength and the sun. Greens, blues and purples are the 'cool' colours as they remind us of gentle things like green fields and still pools of water. That isn't to say if you were painting a picture of a fire that you shouldn't use any cool colours. You could find that by adding a green or a blue flame in contrast to the warm colours, it will give emphasis and make the fire even more lively.

Warm colours always appear to come towards you, cold colours appear to go away. You can use this knowledge to help to give your pictures a feeling of distance.

Notice the effect one colour has on another, too. Look at the diagrams here. The spots of colour are exactly the same. See how they seem to change when they have different coloured backgrounds.

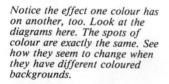

Tone is important when you are using colour. To help you to recognise what tone is, half close your eyes and look around you. Colours will be less noticeable than the darkness or lightness of things. In your paint box too, each colour has its own tone and can help you to make some parts of a picture more important than others. For example, dark figures against a lighter background will really stand out. This is called *contrast* and, with experience, you will learn to use contrasting tones and colours to distinguish every part of your picture. You should not find it necessary to use a dark outline to make parts of your picture clear.

Texture or surface pattern is another important aspect of picture-making as it is yet another way of distinguishing objects from each other. Try painting a picture using one single-toned colour and show the differences in each object by painting their patterns; straight or curly brush strokes for hair, the pattern of the grain in wooden objects, the flat colour of a smooth object, and so on.

7

The *composition* or positioning of the shapes in a picture is very important in order to get the best effect. The arrangement of the objects or shapes in a picture should always be carefully considered. This applies particularly to the main areas of tone or colour; each may eventually contain detail or variations of tone but you should think of the large masses first. By organising these you can lead the viewer's eye round the picture to arrive at the most important point, called the *focal point*. There are many ways of creating a focal point e.g. by use of contrasting colours, light and dark tones or large and small shapes.

These simple diagrams show different ways of leading your eye to the focal point.

The following set of pictures will show how these diagrams can be related to realistic situations.

Of course, these are only a few ways of constructing a picture. Explore for yourself the many endless possibilities.

There are one or two things to avoid. Never split your picture in two by filling up the two sides or the top and bottom leaving the centre empty and devoid of interest.

Avoid cutting your picture in half in any way by a strong continuous line. Try to remember in a realistic painting that your picture has depth as well as height and width. Treat it as if it were a window, framing your chosen subject.

Although most of you will want to paint things you see or remember, there will always be something very personal about your picture. No two people express an idea the same way. Although it is wise to look at the work of other artists, always try to express your own ideas in your painting.

Some people like to think about, and concentrate on, colour. Some people are intrigued by light and shade. Others like to portray pattern or texture. Few artists would be able to give equal value to all these things in one painting.

Although the same objects appear in all these three oil paintings, the pictures were painted by three different artists, each revealing his own style both in the arrangement and in the treatment of the painting.

Gouache Painting

Gouache is the paint most used by designers and can be found in design studios all over the world. It is of the highest quality, the smoothest texture, and it comes in a large range of colours.

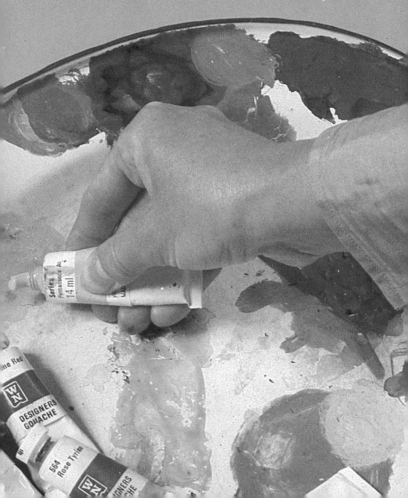

Gouache is mixed with water. Use enough to make it soft and creamy, and thick enough to cover your background. It is an *opaque* paint, meaning that you should not be able to see through it. However, some gouache colours, for example *Golden Yellow*, *Madder Carmine* and *Viridian*, are not opaque in the tube. These can be made opaque by mixing them with other dense colours.

You make gouache paint paler by adding white, whereas water-colour paint is made paler by the addition of water; this dilutes the colour and allows the white paper to show through. This is the major difference between gouache and water-colour paints.

Poster paint is a good substitute for gouache, although it is not such good quality and it dries a little lighter than you expect. It comes in a wide range of colours including gold, silver and bronze. It has a consistency similar to gouache, being thick and creamy, and it is much cheaper to buy. One can obtain Poster Colour in many sizes and styles of containers including tubes, but it can also be bought in hard discs, rather like water colours.

Gouache paint comes in a tube which is coded to show whether it is opaque, whether it will fade after a time, whether it is poisonous, and whether it stains. This type of information is very useful to professional artists and designers, who must always achieve the highest standards. Once you have used this versatile and brilliant paint, I'm sure you will understand its popularity.

WARNING! A few of the colours in the gouache range are slightly poisonous if not used properly, so don't take risks like sucking the hairy end of your brush or mistaking the white paint for your toothpaste!

It is most important that you look after your paints and equipment properly. Always remember to replace the tops on your tubes of paint immediately after use, or your colour will dry out and become rock hard. Squeeze tubes from the bottom so that you don't waste paint or break your tubes.

It is well worth investing in top quality sable hair brushes if you can, as they are long lasting, hardwearing, and strong. If you can only afford one to begin with, then choose either a size four, five or six. It will depend on the size of work you want to do. Of course, a fairly wide range of brushes is necessary even if they are not sable hair. Whatever brushes you choose, you must always clean and store them carefully after use. Wash them carefully in cold water, dry them on a clean rag or tissue and store them either in a jar with their bristles in the air, or prepare a roll of corrugated card, slightly longer than your brushes. Put an elastic band round the roll and store your brushes by pushing them under the elastic band so that they are held tight along the length of the card roll (*see picture below*). This can then be stored in a box.

Gouache can be mixed on any non-absorbent surface. I like to use a flat, white kitchen plate, but you could use a piece of laminated plastic, or a bun tin, where the separate wells might help you to keep your colours clean. Whatever you choose, you need only squeeze out the colours that you know you will be using to start your painting, adding to them from time to time. Try not to waste paint by putting out too many colours at once. You will use much more white than any other colour, so you can afford to be more generous in squeezing that out.

Use a big pot for your water and keep it clean. Muddy water makes muddy colour. When mixing, always clean your brush on a rag or tissue before rinsing it in your water. This prevents your having to change your water quite so often.

To mix your paint, dip a clean brush into the paint and transfer it to another part of the plate, mixing it gently with enough water until it is the right consistency: creamy, not runny. Add other colours to this to achieve the shade you require, always ensuring that there are no streaks in it before you paint.

The quantity of paint you mix depends on the size of area you wish to complete. Experience will help you to make this judgement, but it is better to over estimate the quantity than to find you have run out of a colour. It is hard to match a colour a second time but if you do mix too much you can always add other colours to it and use it elsewhere on your picture.

It is possible to paint on all sorts of surfaces and you often need to spend little or no money on these. Newspaper, though it soaks up water, can present you

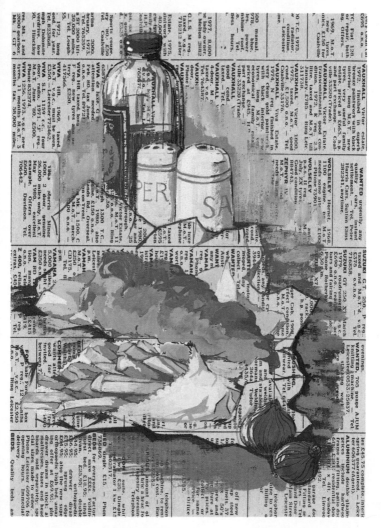

with an interesting background, especially if you paste it smoothly onto a piece of card, leaving it to dry before you start your picture.

Ordinary brown wrapping paper has a warm grainy
surface. If it has been creased it can be easily ironed
before use, to smooth it out.

If you cut scrap paper into a lacy pattern and lay it over another piece of paper, you can make a very attractive design by splattering paint over the surface. Mix plenty of colour and dip an old toothbrush into it. Rub your thumb or index finger over this (or use an old knife or nail file if you prefer) and direct the spray you make over the holes of your pattern, being careful to avoid knocking your paper whilst doing this. When the paint has really covered the holes, remove your lacy paper, called a stencil, and wait for the paint to dry. When the paint is completely dry replace the stencil in a different place, perhaps upside down, mix another colour and splatter the paint again. When it is dry, and you have removed the stencil, you will find an attractive result. Whilst you are doing this work remember to wear an apron and cover the surroundings of your work. It can be a messy job!

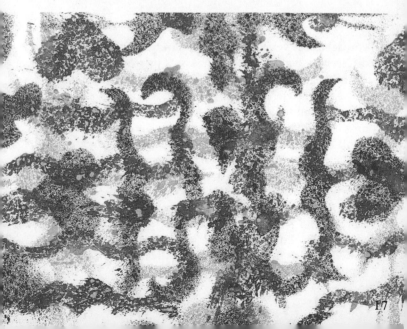

Gouache is a versatile paint. It can be used in all these
different ways and for many kinds of work. Here you
see a landscape, almost finished. You will notice that
before I started, I used a big brush and light paint to
cover all the major areas of my painting. After these
areas were dry, I began to paint the smaller details using
small brushes for the distant items. For the foreground,
I used a palette knife and edges of card dipped into the
paint and printed on the paper. I used warmer colours,
yellows and browns, in the foreground, to help to give
the appearance of its being close to you, but in the
background I used cooler colours to help to give a sense
of distance. The rich colours, the light and shade, the
pattern and texture, were the qualities that I wanted to
capture when I first saw this part of Italy.

I did not need to use a pencil to put down these marks, indeed it would have been a waste of time to draw these small details first, as the paint would have covered them over. Try to avoid drawing any detail with pencil before you start a painting, for the same reasons.

On the record sleeve below I have used the paint in a very different way. After I planned my design, based on the composer's name and the mood of the music, I drew it lightly and carefully with a sharp pencil to be sure that the letters filled the sleeve and were exactly where I wished to place them. Then, using a flat brush, I painted in the big smooth areas of colour, taking care that the edges of this crisp pattern were very straight and neat. This is something you must try to do if you use lettering for posters, notices, or similar work.

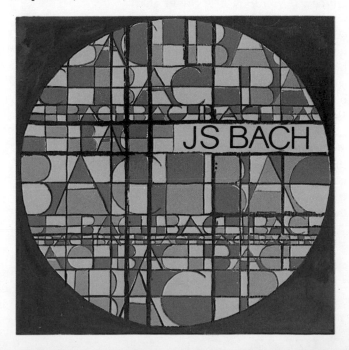

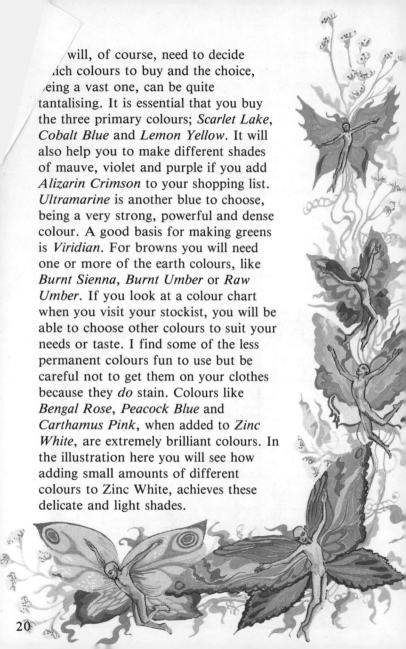

will, of course, need to decide
...ich colours to buy and the choice,
...eing a vast one, can be quite
tantalising. It is essential that you buy
the three primary colours; *Scarlet Lake*,
Cobalt Blue and *Lemon Yellow*. It will
also help you to make different shades
of mauve, violet and purple if you add
Alizarin Crimson to your shopping list.
Ultramarine is another blue to choose,
being a very strong, powerful and dense
colour. A good basis for making greens
is *Viridian*. For browns you will need
one or more of the earth colours, like
Burnt Sienna, *Burnt Umber* or *Raw
Umber*. If you look at a colour chart
when you visit your stockist, you will be
able to choose other colours to suit your
needs or taste. I find some of the less
permanent colours fun to use but be
careful not to get them on your clothes
because they *do* stain. Colours like
Bengal Rose, *Peacock Blue* and
Carthamus Pink, when added to *Zinc
White*, are extremely brilliant colours. In
the illustration here you will see how
adding small amounts of different
colours to Zinc White, achieves these
delicate and light shades.

On the other hand, this painting of a Venetian canal
shows how you can use dark colours to advantage. I put
out the colours I wanted and gradually added black to
many of them. There are three types of black gouache;
Lamp, *Ivory* and *Jet*. If you can only afford one of
these, Jet Black is probably the most useful as it is the
densest of all. When it is lightened with white it makes a
very blue grey. Lamp Black is not quite so dense and it
makes very cool greys. Ivory Black is a warmer,
brownish black and makes good neutral colours which
you will see in the next picture.

...will see neutral colours in nature. Look for example ...ones, wood, moss, bones, shells and earth. This ...nting, a close-up view of a river rushing over some ...ossy stones, uses a great variety of subtle, neutral ...olours. I have mixed white with different blacks, greens and earth colours for this picture.

You will need the other white, *Permanent White*, to help you to lighten your colours, but mainly to thicken them and to help them become opaque, so that they will cover other colours. Normally it is advisable to work in light colours when you begin a picture and gradually apply darker tones. One of the advantages of gouache is that it is possible to cover over mistakes, or to change your mind as you are working.

Certain colours, like *Rose Carthame*, *Viridian Lake* or *Cyprus Green*, are almost impossible to cover. These, and other strongly staining colours will always be difficult to cover over but it is a problem that can be partly solved by using a fixative spray such as *Letraset 103*. A fine spray from this aerosol can will seal the surface of your painting, enough to let you paint over it with varying degrees of success.

The painting you see above is an example of how light colours can be superimposed on a dark ground. I began this work by filling in the background with fairly dark colours, over which I painted this winter pattern.

Gouache's fine texture and rich, silky finish lends itself to use in flat decorative pattern. Most objects in your home which have a flat pattern on them probably started life as designs in gouache on an artist's drawing board.

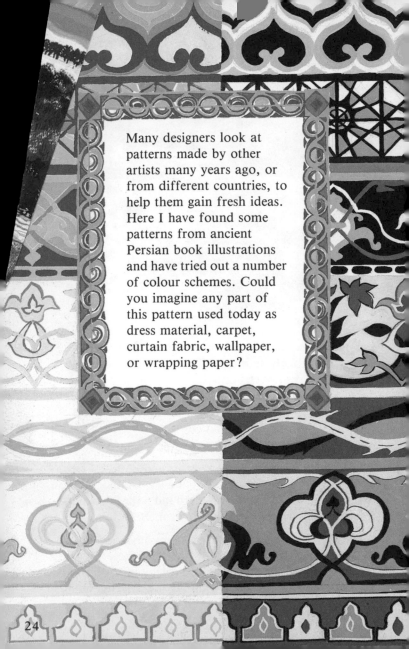

Many designers look at patterns made by other artists many years ago, or from different countries, to help them gain fresh ideas. Here I have found some patterns from ancient Persian book illustrations and have tried out a number of colour schemes. Could you imagine any part of this pattern used today as dress material, carpet, curtain fabric, wallpaper, or wrapping paper?

25

Pets don't often sit still long enough for you to paint them, but if you watch them carefully for a while, you should be able to do a painting of them from memory. Gouache is a good paint to use to show the texture of fur or feathers.

Gouache does not restrict you to any particular style of painting. The important thing is to paint what you feel like painting, to look closely and carefully at the world about you, and not to be disheartened by your mistakes.

If you wish to paint from observation, set yourself a group of objects such as plants, fruit, vegetables or articles in your own home (this is called a *still life*) and try to paint what you see. Do notice that shadow is rarely black, but is a darker version of the colour on which it is falling. Highlights too are not always white.

Few designers today actually produce the article they have designed. They have to put down their ideas clearly so that other people can understand and carry out their plans. A costume designer for television, film or theatre, might well use gouache for his or her designs, as it can easily be used to show the texture of the cloth and trimmings. Can you identify the materials and decorations used in this design? Perhaps you would enjoy painting characters in historical or national costume, or just fantastic beings from your imagination.

Often artists use gouache to prepare their ideas for larger paintings to be carried out in oil paints. Gouache allows them to work faster and on a smaller scale, but gives a general effect of their ideas. This is often the case in portrait painting where an artist likes to get to know the subject thoroughly first.

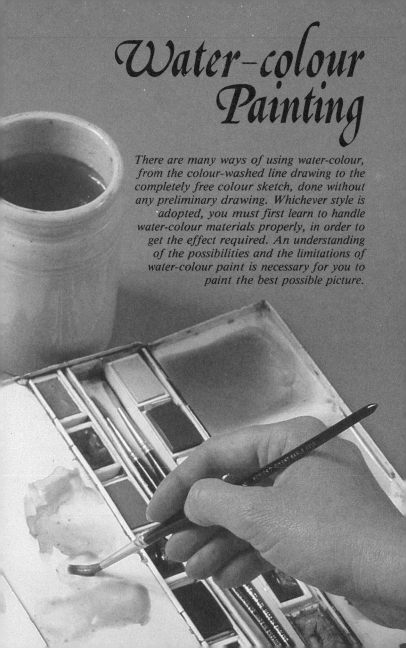

Water-colour Painting

There are many ways of using water-colour, from the colour-washed line drawing to the completely free colour sketch, done without any preliminary drawing. Whichever style is adopted, you must first learn to handle water-colour materials properly, in order to get the effect required. An understanding of the possibilities and the limitations of water-colour paint is necessary for you to paint the best possible picture.

First, let us look at the materials, beginning with the colours. Avoid having too many. This is important for not only is it quite unnecessary, it is confusing. The following list will provide all the colour combinations you will normally need: *Cadmium Yellow Pale*, *Yellow Ochre*, *Raw Sienna*, *Burnt Sienna*, *Vermilion*, *Rose Madder*, *Viridian Green*, *Cobalt Blue*, *Ultramarine Blue*, *Winsor* or *Monastral Blue*.

Choose a paint-box that has plenty of space to mix paint; one with two or three divisions in the lid plus a folding inner palette. One way to do this more cheaply is to buy a large, inexpensive box of paints and to remove the colours and refit the box with artists' colours. Always buy the best colours and brushes you can afford.

As a general rule use the largest brush you can. A number 8 is a good standard size with a 2.5 cm (1″) wide flat brush for laying on washes and skies, and a number 5 or 6 sable for smaller details.

Water-colour papers come in various thicknesses and textures. For quick sketches these are suitable for use as they are. If, however, a large wash is required they must be stretched or they will cockle badly. Damp the paper thoroughly, leave for 5 minutes then stick it down onto your drawing board using brown gummed paper round the edges of the paper. When dry, the paper will be taut.

Hand made papers are excellent to use but rather expensive. It is best to try rougher surfaces as smooth surfaced papers do not retain the paint easily and streaks occur.

Cartridge paper and Ingres paper is easily obtained, but don't be tempted to buy the dark colours available in the

Ingres range as water-colour must always be used on a light ground. Water-colour boards are available and, though they are fairly expensive, they do not require stretching.

Now mix a quantity of colour in the lid of the box, using plenty of water, and place your drawing board on a slight slope. Take a full brush load and, starting in the top left hand corner, draw it straight across the paper (left handed people start top right). Because of the slope of the board the colour will collect at the bottom of the stroke. Now take another full brush load and make another stroke overlapping the wet edge of the first stroke. Repeat this, each time collecting the wet edge of the stroke above, until you have covered the area.

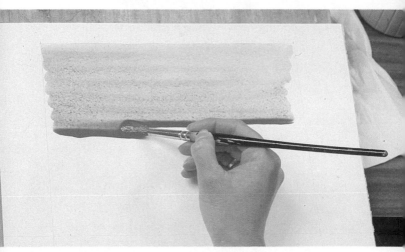

Practise this until you can lay a good wash and then try gradating the colour. Start with clear water and gradually add colour. See what different effects you can obtain in this way.

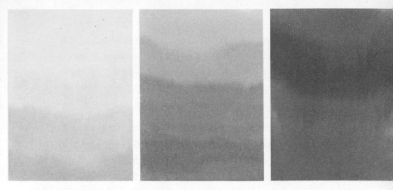

Practise varying the tone of the wash so that you can get used to controlling the paint in various ways. It is impossible to alter a graded wash once it is dry so it is important to learn to control this technique by experimenting with it. Lay on one colour then work another colour or darker tone into it, as you would if you were painting heavy cloud formations.

Try wetting the surface where the soft edge of the shadows will be, then run your colour along this edge so that the colour spreads into the wet area. This will give you a certain type of soft edge. Sometimes a wash of clear water is put over the whole area before the colour is applied, this is called 'floating'.

Although the wash is an essential technique to master, it is also possible to use an almost dry brush to build up shapes or detail. A water-colourist has to learn to work fast. Always mix enough colour for the area you are going to paint. It is very difficult to mix exactly the same colour twice, and if the colour dries on your paper the second application will leave a streak where it overlaps the first.

Water-colour is a transparent medium and white should not normally be used. Pale tones are achieved by the use of water, so these, and any white areas, need to be carefully planned. Corrections are difficult, but some paint can be lifted off by flooding the area with fresh water and soaking it up with a clean tissue, small sponge, or a clean dry brush.

Mistakes can often be avoided if you remember to wait for each area to dry before you paint the next colour. If two wet colours touch, they will run. This, however, can be used deliberately for interesting effects as in this illustration.

34

It is perhaps more important in water-colour than in any other medium, to plan your picture carefully. Draw very lightly with a fairly soft pencil, such as a 2B, and only draw the simplest of guidelines to help you. It is confusing and unnecessary to draw in detail, as too much detailed drawing is often difficult, if not impossible, to erase when the picture is completed.

It is sensible with most paintings to start at the top and work with your drawing board at an angle. This allows the paint to collect at the bottom of each stroke but the board should not be so steep that the colour will trickle accidentally.

You may choose to dampen your paper before you start, to help you to avoid streaks. Paint your washes first, making them paler rather than darker. It is always easier to darken a water-colour, but nearly impossible to lighten it. Never paint detail first.

When you have covered your page with light washes, leaving any white areas you need, you can then start building up smaller areas with slightly darker tones. Leave the fine, dark detail until last. The white of your paper should shine through your colours.

To protect this transparent quality, avoid using any more than three overlapping washes, or your results will look muddy.

Sometimes a water-colour can be more interesting if some fine pen and ink drawing is added to it, as in this painting of Wistow Church, Leicestershire.

With some knowledge and practice in water-colour it would now be useful to study the various stages in producing a painting — in this case, a landscape.

This particular subject by Frank Humphris was chosen because it presents several different exercises in the actual handling of the paint. The sky is an example of 'floating' the colours onto a wet background; the wooded hills are basically flat washes; detail is chosen in the cluster of cottages, while a gradated wash is used on the foreground trees and field.

FRANK HUMPHRIS · 1943

This was a quick holiday sketch in which the pencil drawing was done deliberately to show through the paint. There was no strong light and the form of the cliffs and rocks is indicated by the pencil lines. The paint shows more of the local colours than the shape.

The sand, as well as the cliffs, show examples of how other colours are added as the washes are applied. In the case of the sand this shows the areas still wet.

Three Cliffs Bay, Gower Coast
by Frank Humphris

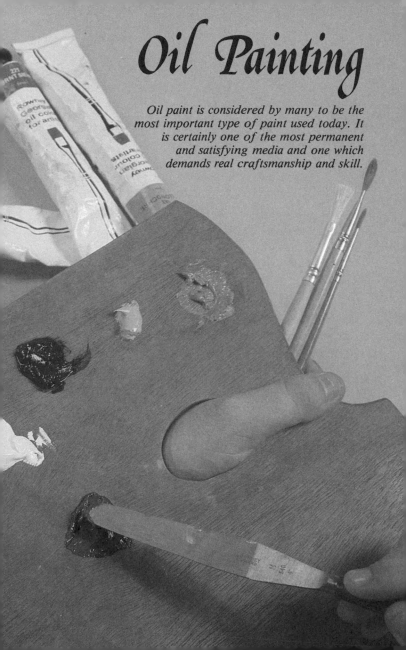

Oil Painting

Oil paint is considered by many to be the
most important type of paint used today. It
is certainly one of the most permanent
and satisfying media and one which
demands real craftsmanship and skill.

Many people, unfortunately, are frightened of the initial outlay needed and this prevents them from painting in oils. This chapter will show you that it is not quite so difficult or expensive to work in oils.

Oil paint cannot be removed easily from clothes or furnishings so you need to make sure that both you and your surroundings are well protected. Your cleaning agent will be a bottle of household turpentine and plenty of rags.

Set up your equipment carefully before you start. Lay things out on the bench or table in an orderly fashion. An easel is not absolutely essential as you can prop your board or canvas against a wall or chairback if they are suitably protected.

You will need two small jars; old aerosol can lids or egg cups will do. This will save you buying a *dipper*, which is a two-welled container used for linseed oil and turpentine. Only buy refined linseed oil and distilled turpentine to use in very small quantities when mixing your paint.

What to paint on
You can paint on any number of surfaces. Canvas, of
course, is the most common, but it is quite expensive.
Plywood is quite a satisfactory base provided it is not
too large. Hardboard is excellent and off-cuts can be
bought quite cheaply. Thick cardboard, coated with glue
size on both sides, will be fairly good. Commercially-
produced boards are usually fairly expensive and their
surfaces are sometimes not well prepared.

Before commencing your work, your board will need
preparing. This is called *priming*. Use ordinary white
undercoat paint (NOT emulsion) and a large brush. Coat
the surface evenly and wait for it to dry. Then apply
another coat and leave to dry thoroughly.

Paint
There are two qualities of oil paint; artists' colour and
students' colour. The former is longer-lasting, refined
and more expensive. Students' colours contain *filler* and
do not go so far although they are cheaper. Perhaps to
start with you would be happier experimenting with the
cheaper quality paint, but as you gain experience and
can afford it, you would be wise to buy artists' quality.

The colours you choose depend very much on your style
or subject matter. It is necessary, however, to buy at
least the three primary colours, plus a large tube of
white and a small tube of black. The bare minimum
could be *Chrome Yellow* or *Lemon Yellow, Cobalt Blue*
or *Ultramarine, Cadmium Red* or *Scarlet, Flake White*
or *Titanium White* and *Ivory Black*. With careful
experimenting you can achieve a range of reds, pinks,
oranges, blues, yellows, greens and neutrals all from
these basic colours.

All these colours and tones were mixed from the three primary colours and black and white.

The other important colours you might then wish to buy might be *Yellow Ochre, Burnt Sienna, Raw Umber* and *Burnt Umber, Alizarin Crimson, Violet, Vermilion* and *Viridian. Zinc White* gives you the cleanest pale tones, whereas *Flake White* is opaque and covers well. There are numerous other colours with which you can experiment. You will decide on those which suit your needs as you gain experience.

The range of colours broadens as other colours are added.

Brushes

Always buy good brushes. They will last longer and improve the quality of your work. You will need both hog hair and sable hair brushes. To begin with, it is advisable to buy the short, square-ended, hog hair brushes. These are called *brights* and are suitable for larger areas and thick paint. For detailed work, you can use either small, round, hog hair brushes or flat-ended sable hair brushes. The size depends on the size of the work you intend to do. One of each of sizes 4, 6, 8 and 10 should suit most beginners. The recommended size of board to work on is approximately 30 cm × 38 cm. It is not advisable to work on less than this when you begin.

This is a selection of oil painting brushes from which you may make your choice.

Palette

The wooden palette is attractive but not essential. A strip of 'Formica', a marble slab or a plain piece of varnished plywood will do. Paper palettes can be bought, but are often rather small. Palette knives are useful and so are painting knives, but a painting knife can serve as both. With it, you can both mix paint and apply it to your pictures.

Before you begin painting, you will need to squeeze out your colours onto your palette. You will usually need more white than any other colour. Most artists put their colours out in some kind of order. I start with white and go through yellow, orange, brown, red, mauve, blue and black. To mix your colours, transfer the fresh colour with a painting knife to the clean centre of your palette and then proceed to mix either with the knife, or with a combination of brush and knife.

Your palette will remain fresh for several days with the addition of a little extra linseed oil dropped onto the paint. Large amounts of unused paint can be scraped off and stored in a jar of water for later use.

Starting to paint

There are basically two ways of working with oil paint. *Glazing:* You need to use a very thin consistency of paint for each layer. This is arrived at by a careful blending of refined linseed oil and distilled turps or white spirit. Each layer of paint must dry thoroughly before another is applied. Drying time varies but can take two or three days, depending on the amount of oil used and on weather conditions. In the mixture of oil and turps there should be slightly more oil than turps. Too much turps will make your work crack.

The other method is to use the paint thickly, either with brush or painting knife. This is certainly a quicker process, though perhaps not as easy to master as glazing.

Some artists combine the two methods, laying in backgrounds and skies with thin paint and gradually increasing the thickness of paint towards the foreground.

As a painting progresses, adjustments can easily be made. It is possible to scrape off wet paint with a palette knife, or painting knife, or to wipe it off with a rag.

The early stages of a painting, after glazing.

*The next stage
is the building up
of colour and detail.*

When paint is dry it can be successfully painted over. Thus mistakes can easily be corrected.

Just as important as setting up your painting kit is its maintenance and care. Do be careful to clean up thoroughly after each session, with special attention to your brushes. Clean them, first by continuously wiping off the excess paint on plenty of rag with a little turpentine. When very little more paint appears on the rag, take your brushes to the sink and rub them gently on some hard soap. With a little water, rub them into a lather on the palm of your hand and rinse them under the tap. Only when no more colour comes out on the soap are your brushes clean enough to be dried and put away. If you know you will be storing hog hair brushes for some time, put a drop of olive oil on the bristles to keep them supple.

The finished painting with the fine detail added.

Having learnt about your materials, you will be thinking about what to paint. This, of course, will be your personal choice. You may wish to paint a still life or a landscape, a portrait or a figure study. You may prefer to rely on your memory or imagination, or you may enjoy a more abstract approach, enjoying colour, line or shape in its own right. You may wish to study the work of famous artists and use some of their approaches to subject matter. Ultimately, the choice is yours.

To begin with though, I would suggest that you keep your work simple. Pay attention to one aspect at a time perhaps. Think about a range of colours and tones, possibly observing plants which have a close range of colours. Try to understand light, shade and tone, noticing how strong tones advance and pale tones recede. Try using a painting knife and paint with it directly onto the board with vigour and life. Van Gogh was a great exponent of this particular technique.

A Cornfield, with Cypresses by Van Gogh
THE NATIONAL GALLERY, LONDON

Attempt nothing that will demand small or delicate details at this stage. Only when you have experimented, and have begun to understand the materials, can you control them to the fine degree needed for detailed work.

Finally a word about varnishing. Do not varnish an oil painting until about 6 months after its completion. Then, make sure it is dust-free, and gently brush on picture varnish with a large, clean, soft-haired brush. Varnish protects work from dust and enlivens the painting.

GLOSSARY OF TERMS

ABSORBENT SURFACE That which soaks up liquid.

BRIGHTS Short, square-ended, hog bristle brushes used for laying on thick oil paint.

COMPOSITION Arrangement and construction of parts of a picture.

CONTRAST Difference of tone, colour or texture that separates parts of a picture.

DIPPER Container to hold oil and turpentine for oil painting.

EASEL Wooden stand for supporting painting in progress.

FILLER Ingredients used to make paint go further.

FIXATIVE Liquid used as a fine spray to stop smudging of pastels etc.

FLOATING Applying water-colour paint to paper already wetted with clean water.

FOCAL POINT Centre of interest in a picture.

GLAZING Oil painting technique whereby thin layers of paint are superimposed on one another.

GLUE SIZE Glue made liquid by addition of hot water. Used to make surfaces non-absorbent.

GRADATE Gradually change shade.

INGRES PAPER (Pronounced 'angra') A paper with a regular grain that has a coloured fleck which gives a mottled effect.

LINSEED OIL Hardening when dry, this oil is used both in the manufacture of paint and the process of oil painting.

NEUTRAL COLOURS Colours which are indeterminate, neither *hot* nor *cold*. Greys and creams etc.

OPAQUE Opposite to transparent; dense, cannot be seen through.

PIGMENT Raw colour.

PRIMARY COLOURS The three pigments which cannot be achieved by mixing i.e. red, blue, yellow.

PRIMING Laying down a first coat of paint to seal a surface for painting.

PERMANENT COLOURS Those which do not fade or deteriorate.

SABLE HAIR Best quality hair used in brushes.

STILL LIFE Group of objects arranged for painting.

TEXTURE The feeling or appearance of a surface.

TONE Light or shade.

TURPENTINE Liquid used to dilute or dissolve wet oil paint.

WASH Flat layer of paint, especially water-colour.